Rose and Rabbit Go to the Fair

WANDA HOWELL

Illustrated by Dillon Olney & Christine Olney

ISBN: 1470181568
ISBN-13: 9781470181567

For My Grandchildren

In everything you do, put God
first, and He will direct you and
crown your efforts with success.

Proverbs 3:6
Living Bible

On a quiet country road not too far from town,

Lived a little old farmer and his wife, rather round.

The farmer worked hard in the fields he plowed,
Keeping ahead of a big rain cloud.

Morning and night he milked cows in his barn,
And his wife knitted sweaters from big balls of yarn.

The farmer enjoyed a comfortable life,
Living on his farm with his hard working wife.

The farmer had a problem though.
He had piles of junk with no place to go.

He never threw anything away,
So on his farm the junk did stay!

There were combines and cars and pickups, too.
Just a whole lot of stuff that might interest you.

Soon the junk filled up a whole feed lot.
There was not even one tiny empty spot!

One warm afternoon,
I think it was June,

The farmer's friendly old dog named Rose
Was following a rabbit by using her nose.

Rabbit hopped into a pickup and sat on the seat.
Rose got in too, to get out of the heat.

The chase was over but they began to plan.
"Let's drive this old pickup truck if we can."

Rose put on an old hat and got behind the wheel.
And then, my goodness, how the tires did squeal!

Away they went, the two friends from the farm.
The old pickup truck was running like a charm.

Out onto the highway went the pair.
They headed down the road straight to the Fair.

They saw a large crowd when they got there,
But they blended right in so no one would stare.

Rose noticed a big sign that read "Dog Show",
And sure enough, she decided she should go.

She entered the competition just like that,
And looked pretty grand wearing her hat.

When the judging was all over and done,
It appeared that Rose really had won!

A beautiful blue ribbon was the prize,
And, my oh my, it was just the right size.

It seemed to the pair that the day was done.
They surely had enjoyed a great deal of fun.

Rose and friend Rabbit jumped into the truck.
Arriving safely back home would be their good luck.

Rose said to her friend as they turned into the lot,
"I think I'll show Farmer this ribbon I got!"

That's all for this time.

Wanda Howell is a busy wife, mother and grandmother. She is a fabric artist who designs and pieces quilts. Wanda and her husband live near Columbia City, Indiana with an orange cat named Nelson. This is her first book for children.

Dillon Olney grew up in Fort Wayne, Indiana. He has been drawing for as long as he can remember. He is currently pursuing a BFA degree in sculpture at Indiana University in Bloomington, Indiana, hoping to one day become a professor of art.

Christine Olney is a graduate of The Ohio State University. As an artist, she finds her inspiration in her family. She was pleased to be asked by her son, Dillon, to add her unique touch to the Rose and Rabbit project.